# THE SECRET LIFE OF SPINSTERS

## DESIRING THE DEXINGTONS
### BOOK TWO

# RENEE DAHLIA

# FOREWORD

Welcome to THE SECRET LIFE OF SPINSTERS, the second book in the Desiring the Dexingtons series.

The Dexington family owns a linen factory in Manchester and consists of Humphrey Dexington and his seven sisters. The Secret Life of Spinsters is the story of Elspeth Dexington.

If you love rich girl/poor girl sapphic romances, this one should appeal.

Please note this novella includes mentions of slavery, the Luddite movement, and adoption.

This book is written in Australian English and some spelling and phrases may be unfamiliar to American readers.

If you are keen to keep up to date on new releases and, more importantly, sales, I recommend you sign up to my newsletter at www.reneedahlia.com.

I hope you enjoy reading this book!

Renée

# ABOUT THE AUTHOR

An avid reader, Renée Dahlia writes contemporary and historical queer romance. Renée is a bisexual cis woman who is fascinated by people and loves to explore human relationships, with a side of humour, through her writing. Renée has a degree in physics and mathematics, using this to write data-based magazine articles for the horse racing industry. Her love of horses often shines through in her fiction, and she loves a good intrigue and to escape the real world in the pages of a book. When she isn't reading or writing, Renée spends her time with her four children, usually watching them play cricket.

# THE SECRET LIFE OF SPINSTERS

*An unexpected alliance between spinsters...*

Confirmed spinster ELSPETH DEXINGTON works in the Dexington family linen manufacturing business dealing with logistics. She believes that machinery will make clothing cheaper for the people, and therefore everyone can afford new clothes, not hand-me-downs and turned cuffs. But when her father declares they will stop manufacturing linen and shift to cotton, she has a new fight on her hands. Producing affordable clothing shouldn't come at such a great human cost.

Help comes in an unexpected form. FLORENCIA WAULKER is the daughter of one of the Luddite organisers. She does all her blind father's correspondence, but when he orders an attack on the Dexington factory, she realises his belief in the need to rid factories of machines has gone too far. She sneaks out to warn the daughter of the factory owner, only to find herself caught up in a conspiracy.

Can two spinsters work together to prevent a disaster, or two? Or is falling in love the real problem?

# CHAPTER ONE

**E**lspeth hated waiting. And waiting for a man... impossible. To be fair, her entire life revolved around waiting for men. At this very minute, she was waiting for Father. He was about to make a business decision that she would likely be pressed to implement, and since it was a decision she really, really, didn't agree with, she was also waiting for her brother. Humphrey would, surely, talk some sense into Father. Tensions in Manchester were high after the lethal Luddite demonstration nine weeks ago, exacerbated by the assassination of Prime Minister Perceval, and while all of that was deeply concerning, those issues were the least of her worries given Father's latest idea to expand into the dreaded cotton business. Cotton, produced by slaves in the new world, wasn't a product she wanted to be associated with.

"Are you coming?" Her oldest sister, Prudence, poked her head into Elspeth's room.

"Where?"

"To the docks. Mr Chan arrives today with a new shipment of silks from China." Prudence had married Mr Chan, one of their fabric traders, over a decade prior and Pru ran the Manchester arm of his import business whenever he was away on a purchasing trip to China, while also running their household and looking after their four children. One of the Dexington factories took the silks Mr Chan imported and created home furnishing such as matching cushion sets.

"Of course." It was better than sitting here waiting for a letter from Humphrey. It'd been weeks since she'd written to Humphrey about her current dilemma and she had no idea if he hadn't responded because he was a busy man, or because the post was unreliable, or some other reason. The uncomfortable truth was that she needed to take this situation in hand herself. She understood the economic argument; cotton was cheaper than linen and that made the cloth more affordable for more people, thus increasing the market. But at what cost? There was no ethical source of cotton. Everywhere in the known world it was grown and picked with the use of slave labour or as they liked to call it in India, indentured labour, which amounted to the same thing. The vast human cost of cotton wasn't worth the benefit of cheaper clothing to others.

"Come on then. The mail arrived with notice that his ship docked at Liverpool. He will be here soon."

Prudence's urgency to be reunited with her husband

prevented Elspeth from schooling her older sister on the fact that she well understood that the mail took four hours to arrive from Liverpool via stagecoach, and cargo took upwards of sixteen hours along the Bridgewater Canal. She performed such calculations daily, while also ensuring the cost per tonne per hour remained low enough to give the Dexington factories a profit margin of note.

"Miss Dexington. A Miss Waulker is here to see you." Ushnish, their butler, stood rigid in the hallway.

"Here?" People didn't visit her at the family house, particularly strangers. She only gave her address to her closest friends, those few who could be trusted into her inner circle.

"Yes. I informed her you would be at your office all day tomorrow, but she insisted she needed to meet you specifically. Here." Ushnish managed to communicate how uncomfortable this odd behaviour made him feel without so much as an eyebrow twitch. He ran their chaotic loud household with aplomb and had done for decades. The grey streaks through his black hair were certainly due to the difficulty of his task. Father, one brother and seven sisters made up the Dexington family. Dear Mama had died in childbed twelve years ago. Prudence, Mr Chan, and their four children lived next door, while her other married older sisters, Hyacinth and Imogen, lived nearby and often visited the main family home. Humphrey, her brother, had left home years ago to make his own fortune in a scandal that never failed to remind Elspeth to be incredibly careful about her own desires.

"Sorry, Pru. I suppose I need to meet this Miss Waulker.

I'll try and make the meeting quick and will head down to the docks on horseback when I'm done."

Prudence squeezed her hands and nodded, a silent acknowledgement that Mr Chan's ship might not make it. Shipping was so risky. Prudence was so brave to keep watching her beloved husband sail away to the other side of the world for business, never knowing if he'd be back or when. Months passed without any communication and no one ever knew if it was because the ship was lost, or because travel took a long time. Even today's message that his ship had docked could be an error. All it would take was someone to read the flag on the incoming ship incorrectly, or for the message to be muddled by the pony rider whose job it was to take the shipping messages from Liverpool to Manchester.

"I'll always be here for you and your children, Pru. You know that." It was her role as the confirmed spinster. She held back a sigh at the uncomfortable thought. Bitterness at the role she'd been thrown in this life shouldn't be a reason to lash out at Pru, especially when she was worried for her husband. Women with her desires didn't find love. There would be no wife for her, not in this society. No one to worry about her when she worked or travelled. No one to hold her hand when she was upset or worried. It wasn't fair. But it was.

"Thank you, my dear. I must make haste." Pru swept down the hallway, leaving Elspeth to stand awkwardly beside Ushnish. Once one of the footmen ushered Pru out the front door and into her carriage, Elspeth finally let out the sigh.

"I can inform Miss Waulker that you are busy."

Elspeth shook her head at Ushnish's tone. "I take it she

refused to budge when you made your first attempts to dismiss her."

"Yes. A determined type."

A little intrigue blossomed in Elspeth's breast. "Introduce me." She followed Ushnish towards the drawing room and waited until he walked through the door before following him. At her entry, there was a bustle of fabric; a heavy rough calico from India by the rough sound of it. Elspeth blinked twice, unable to do more than stare at the paragon of beauty standing in her drawing room. Somehow the adornment of the cheapest painted calico only enhanced her glorious figure. Like so many living in industrial cities, Miss Waulker had mixed heritage, perhaps from the same regions of Asia as Pru's Mr Chan, although Elspeth would be so rude as to never ask. Miss Waulker's wide brown eyes were a dark pool of emotion that Elspeth could easily lose herself in for hours; they shimmered with a quiet intelligence. But it was the way her plump lips were pinched tight as if she were frustrated at having to wait for her that made Elspeth want to giggle. The look she sent Elspeth offered the possibility of her being a most delightfully challenging conversationalist.

"Thank you, Ushnish. That will be all." At her dismissal, slightly ruder than she would usually offer the beloved family butler, he bowed and left the room, closing the door with an audible click that conveyed exactly how he felt about the matter. She would apologise later. For now, she had an audience with a most surprising guest.

# CHAPTER TWO

If her father knew where she was—consorting with one of his many self-elected enemies—Florencia would be locked in his house for months. She could feel the spittle flying from his rant already, even though he had no clue to her current whereabouts. Father might be blind, yet he saw everything and knew everything. It'd been the work of years to know his schedule precisely enough to understand exactly when she might leave the house without his knowledge. Once a week, he had a two-hour appointment with his physician, and it was the one time she was banned from his presence and could guarantee that he wouldn't randomly call for her. She'd tested this for years before taking the risk of leaving, slowly leaving for longer and longer periods during that two hours, and he hadn't noticed yet.

"Miss Waulker. What brings you here?" Miss Dexington asked. Florencia cringed at the censure in Miss Dexington's voice and stared at the handwoven expensive rug on the floor cataloguing every detail of the pattern, instinctually performing the task in case she would be required to describe it later.

She could barely believe she stood in the same room as the intelligent Miss Dexington. She'd read every single word of her weekly column with The Manchester Gentlewoman, all the notes from the Manchester Women's Guild, and committed many of her phrases to memory. It'd been Father who'd encouraged her at first, because she'd read him an advertisement for the column in the Daily. Twice a day, the morning and evening editions, she read the entire newssheet aloud to him. Every single word. That day, he'd wanted her to subscribe to The Manchester Gentlewoman and tell him everything she discovered about the Dexington family. They owned several of the largest mills in town, and Father liked to know everything about all the manufacturing families, from the richest to the smallest operations. He liked to know who paid their workers properly, who had safe working conditions, and who needed help in improving the way they treated their labour force—help—she almost scoffed aloud. Father was one of the leaders of the Luddite movement. His supposed help wasn't always in everyone's best interests, nor was it often above board. It was complex; working conditions needed to be improved and often that only happened when people fought for the workers. When the fight went wrong, like the recent shooting of protestors, she doubted if the fight was worth it. She swallowed and tried to stop her brain running away with itself because the truth was Florencia had run out of time. The butler had left her waiting in here for too long.

The physician would be finished with Father shortly, leaving her barely enough time to convey her message and return home before he realised her absence.

"I'm so sorry." She cleared her throat and forced her gaze up from the floor. Immediately her gaze locked with the deep blue eyes of Miss Dexington. She froze momentarily, then slowly took in the vision before her, automatically taking in everything about her so she could describe her. The habit—being Father's eyes—never went away, even in the rare moments when she was alone. Miss Dexington was what folk called black Irish; pale white skin, with hair so black it almost glowed with a purple light. Adorned in a cream day gown with dark green trimmings, Miss Dexington wore the latest fashions with an ease that could only come from complete self-assurance. Only someone rich could wear a gown of such a pale colour without worrying about keeping it clean. A tiny niggle in the back of Florencia's brain wanted to laugh at the absurdity of the phrase black Irish; they lived in a busy manufacturing town with people from around the globe and the idea that someone with skin so white might be called black made no sense to her. It could only be due to her black hair, somehow even blacker than her own.

"What are you sorry about?" Miss Dexington's calm voice reminded her of her task. She was here to protect Miss Dexington, not admire her elegant form. An unusual sensation built in her chest, an unexpected warmth.

"I have rather urgent news. There is a plot against the Dexington factory on Main Street."

"A plot?"

"Yes." Florencia clenched her jaw. She really shouldn't be here, but this was Miss Dexington who she greatly admired. Of more importance, she didn't want anyone else to get hurt. There had been enough death already. "On Friday next, there is a plan to plant explosives in the north corner of the factory and ignite them. Please don't ask how I know." She picked up her skirts and fled from the room having delivered her message.

"Wait."

"I can't. I have no time."

"You can't say something like that and then leave."

Florencia knew she was being rude, but if Father called for her after his appointment and she didn't respond, he would know she left the house without telling him. She needed to run home, now, before she was caught. The details wouldn't matter to him; he'd feel deeply betrayed by her choice to tell Miss Dexington anything.

"I can and I must. Please. Take heed of my warning."

"Wait. I need more information."

Florencia couldn't refuse Miss Dexington. She only knew her from her writings and yet after only a few minutes in her presence, Miss Dexington was so real to her that she knew she'd take all manner of outrageous risks to protect her.

"Twice a day, every day, I go to the Horse and Hops Inn to collect and deliver Father's correspondence. Meet me there for the mail coach. Be in disguise." Florencia pushed open the front door, checked the street for anyone who might recognise her, then fled before Miss Dexington could speak again. She walked as fast as she could without drawing attention to herself. The notion that anyone knew who she was, or cared, was quite absurd, but Father had a wide network and she couldn't risk him knowing what she'd done. Guilt threatened to overwhelm her. Father didn't deserve to have her undermine him like this; he'd taken her in from the workhouse when she was only a small orphan and given her a good life. With big gulping breaths, she rested on the back gate of their small townhouse until her heart stopped galloping. Once she walked inside, she needed to be completely calm, or Father would know. He'd literally hear the change to her breathing patterns and question her until she confessed, and she could never lie to him. Not in so many words. Lying by omission was a skill she was well crafted in and one that weighed heavily on her conscience.

Hours later, her heart still fluttered erratically whenever she thought of the risks she'd taken this morning. The anticipation of seeing Miss Dexington again only made her pulse race faster. It was all rather untoward.

"Father, was there anything else you want while I deliver this afternoon's correspondence?"

"No. I'm expecting a visitor with the stagecoach today or tomorrow."

"Mr Peyton? Yes, I recall." Please don't be today; not while there was an outside chance Miss Dexington might also be at the staging inn. She would have to snub Miss Dexington in favour of Father's guest. They barely knew each other. It shouldn't matter if Miss Dexington had a poor opinion of her.

"Good. Please let the inn know to put his room on my charge." Father had a small five percenter fund that kept them both adequately fed and housed. For years, Florencia had managed the household accounts, or at least, she'd kept the records that Father dictated. She was literally his eyes in a world that wasn't set up for a blind man to easily navigate, and she knew, deep down, that he had only adopted her from the workplace for that role. The reality of that didn't matter, she loved him for his generous care in making her his daughter. He didn't have to do that. This was a much better life than an orphaned girl could have expected and she was grateful for the chance. Her prospects in the workhouse had been dim. Even at the tiny age of five or six, she'd known her options were to become a servant or a courtesan, and either option would have ended her education then. Father had literally rescued her from a life of poverty, continued to educate her so she could write all his letters and read to him— ultimately he had given her a good middle class life—and her only duty was to assist him. They could afford to employ a cook, Mrs Jones, who came by the house once a day to make bread and dinner; and a maid of all work, Ella, who came four days a week and the two women had become Florencia's friends in her narrow world.

"No. The mail is sufficient. Keep me informed with regards Mr Peyton."

"Yes, Father." Florencia tucked her ancient coat around her to protect against the unseasonably cold wind she'd encountered earlier in the day. According to the newssheets, spring had been the coldest on record since 1799, and with the cold continuing into summer, many rural writers were worried for the harvest yields. Prices would likely rise, and she'd already spoken to Father about how they might manage the household budget if that happened. She picked up the letters they'd written this afternoon and opened her mouth to make an excuse for the extra time she might need, but closed it again when nothing rational came.

"Was there something else?" How Father managed to hear her hesitation never ceased to amaze her.

"No. I think I'm nervous..." She blurted.

"About Mr Peyton. Yes, I suppose the prospect of meeting a stranger would cause some nerves."

Florencia didn't consider herself to be a simpering sheltered miss, yet she barely left the house except for Father's errands. "I'm unaccustomed to company."

"It does worry me. Sending you into the harsh world as a grown women. Have I done enough to ensure your safety?" It was so odd to hear Father express a lack of confidence that she felt a little faint. She ought to be drawn and quartered for betraying his trust. He cared for her and she was a terrible daughter to want more than the quiet steady life he'd given her.

"Father. You have taught me many lessons in resilience and I'm sure I will find the necessary confidence to adjust to any circumstance."

"Yes." He preened a little. "I have faith in your abilities. Mr Peyton wouldn't dare take advantages, although I do wonder if I ought not think more about how to better protect you. Mrs Jones might be the right person to ask about such matters." Father fobbed all womanly issues onto their cook, and she'd long ago learned not to bother him and simply go directly to her.

"I will ask her advice before I leave."

"Good. Stay safe, Florencia." Father cared about her and she was about to meet someone who would undermine his plans. Guilt weighed heavily on her. Once she left the room, she allowed herself a small sigh. There was a good reason to talk to Miss Dexington; Manchester didn't need any more violence. If the Luddites blew up a factory, there would be more retribution and several of Father's acquaintances had already been hurt last time the Luddites clashed with the soldiers who represented the local business owners and government.

# CHAPTER THREE

Elspeth shouldn't let her curiosity get the better of her, yet here she was in the Horse and Hops Inn with her nine-year-old niece Georgia, in disguise, waiting for Miss Waulker to explain her jaw-dropping revelation about the supposed plot to bomb one of the Dexington factories. She barely had time to wonder much when Miss Waulker slid into their booth. From the way she flicked her glance around the room, then settled with her back to the front door, and tightened her bonnet closer to her face, it was more than obvious that she was nervous about being here.

"Good afternoon." Elspeth needed to understand more about the plan against the Dexington factories, so she aimed for her most welcoming tone.

"I don't have very long."

"I assumed so. This is my niece, Miss Georgia Chan. Georgia, this is Miss Waulker. We have some business to discuss."

"Hello, Miss Waulker. Is your Papa from China, like mine? My Papa arrived home today."

Miss Waulker fidgeted a little in her chair.

"I'm terribly sorry. Georgia is very young and she is still learning how to go on in conversation." Elspeth had offered to bring Georgia with her today to give Pru and Mr Chan some time along together after nearly eighteen months apart. The younger children were in the care of Ushnish and the rest of the staff at the main Dexington house.

"No, it's fine. The truth is I'm uncertain of my parentage. I was adopted by my Father from a workhouse." To be adopted out of such difficult circumstances made Miss Waulker incredibly fortunate. The outcome for girls born into the workhouses were usually terrible, which was why Elspeth made a concerted effort to find jobs for them in the Dexington factories so they had options for their futures. Elspeth painted on her most neutral expression.

"I'm so sorry to have allowed an uncomfortable topic to be raised."

"You weren't to know, and your niece is only being naturally curious. I don't imagine she sees someone who looks similar to her very often."

Elspeth frowned. "What are you talking about? There are several Chinese families around here. We've always made an effort for Georgia and her siblings to have a connection to her Father's culture, especially as he travels back there a lot for business. Would you like an introduction?" Elspeth paused as Miss Waulker's cheeks reddened. "I'm so sorry. Please tell me to stop. I have a tendency to leap into other people's business and try to solve their problems."

"I... Thank you for your offer. I must decline." Miss Waulker cast her gaze low, then slowly raised her head with a glowing fierceness in her dark brown eyes. In any other circumstance, Elspeth might wonder if the sparkle included lust, however, she was most likely imagining it. Just because she found Miss Waulker rather lovely, didn't mean her desires were returned. She needed to keep to the topic at hand.

"About this plot you mentioned?"

"Is it?" Miss Waulker glanced at Georgia who was carefully drawing in a notebook with crayons.

"Yes. You can speak freely in front of Georgia. She might be young, however, she's been learning about the family businesses since she could write."

"It's nice to see your writings being put into practice." Miss Waulker hesitated, just long enough for Elspeth to comprehend that Miss Waulker had been reading her weekly column in The Manchester Gentlewoman. "Please be careful on Friday next."

"You refer to the plot against our factory? How did you find out about it?"

"I can't talk about that. I came across details during some correspondence I was doing."

"Someone wrote you a letter about it?"

"Not me. Father." Miss Waulker's countenance paled. "I'm sorry. I've said too much. Please take the threat seriously. I don't want anyone to get hurt."

"You are worried about our factory workers?"

"Yes. And your family, and everyone." Miss Waulker squared her shoulders and Elspeth waited for her to find her courage. "There has been enough death in this labour dispute already. I want this plot stopped and I don't want those who made the plot hurt either."

"I'm not sure that's realistic. People can't plot to blow up a business and expect to pretend it never happened."

"If it doesn't happen, then it is no one's fault. Can you just ensure it is stopped without... Wait. There is a good reason to keep this quiet." Intelligence gave Miss Waulker's gaze a sheen that made Elspeth's heart skip a beat. If they weren't on opposing sides, she would like to get to know Miss Waulker a lot better.

"There is?"

"Yes. If you make a martyr of the people behind this plot, the tensions will only escalate. I came to you to try and prevent more death."

"You keep talking about death."

Miss Waulker's eyes narrowed. "You can't be so sheltered as to live in Manchester and not be aware that of the terrible shootings of Luddites in Yorkshire only a few months ago."

"A terrible day." Elspeth didn't understand the Luddites opposition to their mill—they needed people to train in their use—but she definitely understood that an uprising in one manufacturing town could easily led to one near her family's factories.

"And one we have a chance to stop happening again. I know we are opposites sides of this argument—"

"We are?" Elspeth had already guessed as much but asked

the question to give herself some time to disguise any obvious reaction to the fact that Miss Waulker said as much aloud. "Oh, I see. You must have Luddite connections if you read this plot in some correspondence. How do I know it's not you who is plotting and this conversation—that you wanted to keep secret, I might add..." Elspeth took a deep breath and leaned forward deliberately. "Are you here as a subterfuge to distract me from what is really planned?"

"How dare you? I've risked a lot to come here and warn you." Miss Waulker stood up and hustled out of the pub. Elspeth was left with a sense of confusion and betrayal; how could Miss Waulker throw out such information without any further details and then just leave before she got to the important part.

"Aunt Elspeth?"

"Yes, Georgia?"

"Is something bad going to happen?"

"I'm not sure."

"You'll stop it, won't you? Papa has just come home. I don't want anything bad to happen."

"Nothing bad will happen. Miss Waulker is confused."

"And if she's not? Will you make certain?"

Elspeth squeezed her niece's hand. "I will. I think the first thing we need to do is find out exactly who Miss Waulker is and why she is worried enough to talk to me about it." The most likely source of these letters would be through whoever employed Miss Waulker. She had ink stains on her fingers, so it would make sense that Miss Waulker wrote the correspondence on behalf of her employer.

"We could go to the workhouse and find her Papa."

"We could." Perhaps Miss Waulker's father might know who employed her. There was a mystery at foot and nothing excited Elspeth more than having a problem to solve. "Come along then. To the workhouse we go."

# CHAPTER FOUR

With the Friday bombing soon approaching, Florencia flinched when someone knocked at the door. For the past few days, Mr Peyton had been energetic as he'd organised everything required for the big demonstration —as he called it—although for her, all it amounted to was a parade of people through their front door all requiring tea and refreshments. More people than Florencia had ever entertained in their humble abode, and she was tired of the pretence. Didn't they all realise the potential cost? Not just to the people who might be hurt, but also to the Luddite movement. Coming so soon after the last protest, one where people had been shot, they'd be branded as rebels, foolish people who could only see destruction as a means of preventing technological change. If Father truly wanted change; to see workers gain reasonable rights, safe working conditions, enough money to live on, a halt to children working in unsightly and unsafe conditions; they couldn't let the movement become tarred with destruction. Florencia supported Father's drive for change, she just wasn't sure about the methodology Mr Peyton wanted to employ.

The knock came at an inopportune time as she was currently reading the morning paper to Father, and he didn't like to be interrupted in his intake of the news. Florencia laid down the paper with a quick apology that she would see who was at the door and be back to continue. She opened the front door to see Miss Dexington standing on the front step.

"May I come in?"

"No."

"Who is it?" Father's voice boomed down the hallway.

Miss Dexington leaned in close enough that Florencia could smell her gentle rosewater perfume. "Let me in. I request an audience with your father." Miss Dexington's whisper sent a ripple of warm air down her spine.

"I will ask." Florencia needed time to work out what to do. Nothing good could come from Miss Dexington meeting Father, and her skin went clammy as she realised that Miss Dexington might know too much. She must have connected Father and herself to the planned demonstration in two days. Florencia should never have gone to warn her. She stood outside the drawing room and wiped her hands on her skirts.

"Father. A Miss Dexington is here. She has requested a meeting with you."

His eyebrows rose. "How intriguing. Please bring her in."

"Yes, Father." Florencia had thirteen steps in which to figure out how to manage this situation. Her mind stayed stubbornly blank. "Miss Dexington, Father will see you now."

She held up her hand and beckoned Miss Dexington closer so she could whisper. "Please be warned. Father is completely blind and so the introductions may be different to how it works in the society you are accustomed to."

Miss Dexington only nodded, and stepped backwards, leaving Florencia with a vague warm patch where Miss Dexington's breath had breezed against her neck. She wanted to press her hand against her own skin to keep the feeling close.

"This way, Miss Dexington." Instead, she squared her shoulders and braced herself for what was likely to be a difficult conversation. "Father, Miss Dexington is here to see you. Shall I get some tea?"

"No, thank you." Miss Dexington stood in the centre of the room.

"Please sit. We don't worry about ceremonies here." Florencia waved to a chair and hoped Miss Dexington would sit without arguing. Father liked to have guests close enough that he could hear their breathing; it helped him understand their reactions when he couldn't see their expressions. Naturally Miss Dexington sat elegantly on the chair, seemingly at home in their small house. The light didn't matter to Father and Florencia preferred to keep the curtains open to bring in as much light as possible through their small windows. It made all the reading she had to do much easier on her eyes. The huge bright space of Miss Dexington's drawing room had left her in awe—imagine sitting in that space all day to read.

"It is a pleasure to meet you, Mr Waulker."

Father made a noise like a muffled scoff. "What brings a Dexington to our cottage? I take it this is not a social visit."

"I see you are not someone to bother with the standard politeness." Miss Dexington appeared amused at Father's brash comment, rather than the flush of shame Florencia felt at her Father being so rude.

"Florencia. Since she sees me, Miss Dexington finds me at a disadvantage. Pray, tell me her expression." Father continued his obvious plan to stop Miss Dexington feeling at ease. Florencia tried to send Miss Dexington an apology in her glance, but Miss Dexington only nodded, presumably giving Florencia permission to answer Father.

"She has a pleasing countenance and is dressed in the latest fashions as described in the advertisements on page thirty. Her expression is one of..." Florencia paused to find the right words to describe the beauty before her. Miss Dexington couldn't be described as a sum of her parts; her clever gaze made the rest of her shine.

"Stop prevaricating, child."

"It is a neutral expression, Father."

"Tell me, Miss Dexington with the neutral expression, do you agree with Florencia's description?"

"Of myself?" Miss Dexington asked. "Yes, she has the right of it. If I were continue with the same flavour of honesty as you've shown, I would say I have some curiosity about you."

"About me?"

"Yes. You are the 'humble walker', aren't you?" For Miss Dexington to know how Father signed all his letters to the papers nearly had Florencia gasping. She managed to halt the intake of breath before Father might hear it.

"I am. You have done your research." Father scowled and Florencia waited for the vitriol he would likely throw in her direction. She was often his emotional outlet, and she'd long ago learned not to take it personally. Only now, when she was at fault, did she realise how much resentment she'd built up against him for using her like that. Never once had he apologised for his angry outbursts; instead he expected her to listen and then help him craft his thoughts into a letter to the papers. Miss Dexington glanced at Florencia with such care that she immediately corrected her thoughts, pushing the resentment aside because Father had given her a safe home, and a better life than she could possibly have had without him adopting her. If she had to bear the brunt of his frustration with the world, it was a small price to pay on the scale of things.

"Before you blame your daughter for a leak in information—" Miss Dexington's clarity had her gasping. How dare she state what she'd done in such blatant terms!

"Florencia?"

"Father, I'm sure Miss Dexington means that my loyalty to you is obvious." Oh dear, now she was laying down the guilt a bit thick. Surely he would know that she had told Miss Dexington of the plans to disrupt her family's factory.

Miss Dexington raised a quizzical brow in her direction. "All I know are the simple facts of the situation. Until I arrived here, I had no idea that the humble walker was blind, and by extension I couldn't have known until I walked into this room that Miss Waulker obviously assists you with your correspondence. I only wanted to reassure you that I had the information about you from a Mr Peyton."

"Ahh, young Mr Peyton."

"We caught him creeping around one of our factories late last night and our security took him to lockup."

"I suppose he felt he could get himself out of trouble by informing you of his apparent network." Father didn't seem surprised at the revelation.

"Apparent?"

"Florencia. What is Miss Dexington's expression now?"

Florencia blinked. "A little surprised. Her head is tilted a fraction to the left as if she is calculating her next move. Her lips—" Florencia really didn't want to describe Miss Dexington's very kissable lips to Father. Kissable. Oh. Oh dear. It wasn't just admiration she felt for Miss Dexington's mind. Since she'd first seen her, she'd begun to spin fantasies about kissing Miss Dexington. It could only be fantasies; Mrs Jones' might have mentioned that her sister lived with another woman as if they were married but she'd also emphasised that it was a highly unusual situation and they had to be careful in society. Miss Dexington would never—could never—since her family was so prominent in Manchester. It was pure foolishness to even allow herself to consider such an option, and besides she could never leave Father who needed her.

"Florencia." Father's censure pulled her back to the real world.

"Her lips were a little pinched until I started to describe her expression and now they are parted a fraction and her eyes, well, if I were cynical, I'd say her eyes are dancing with glee because my description gives her time to collect her thoughts and plan a solid rebuttal."

"An intelligent adversary then."

"Mr Waulker. I am not your adversary. I came to visit to discuss our next move with regards to Mr Peyton as I believe we can find a solution that benefits both the Luddite movement and the Dexington businesses."

Father leaned back in his chair. "I take it you expect to use Mr Peyton as a bargaining tool for the Dexington gain and you wish to involve myself to smooth over any potential uprising from your workers. Please leave now. There is nothing I can do for you."

"Are you so determined to believe the worst in me?" Miss Dexington didn't appear upset, only mildly bemused.

"There is little to believe. If the Dexington family was truly taking this matter seriously, they wouldn't have sent a woman for the task. Your presence here merely serves to demonstrate that Mr Dexington wishes to brush this incident under the carpet, so to speak, and paint Mr Peyton as someone working alone."

"Is that the outcome you wish? For Mr Peyton to take all the blame in the press?"

"No. Change doesn't happen quietly."

Miss Dexington smiled. "That's rather an ironic statement coming from a Luddite, given the way the Luddites refuse to acknowledge technological change."

"You misunderstand the motives of our group."

"If that is true, then it is only because you have failed to communicate them properly."

Father's fingers gripped the edge of his chair. "Perhaps you lack basic reading comprehension."

"I doubt that. The humble walker writes pretty words about labour laws and unfairness, and yet the papers all interpret that with respect to the actions of your group. No amount of pretty words can take away from the truth that the Luddites are responsible for many destructive actions. If the goal, as in your letters, is to improve working conditions and teach people how to adjust to change, why wreck the very machines that employ them? Why send Mr Peyton to blow up a factory?"

"You wouldn't understand."

"Because I'm a woman, or because I'm a Dexington?" The way Elspeth spoke to Father, as if she were an equal, bemused by his comments, was so different to the deference everyone else who visited gave him. Father wouldn't like this at all. He was accustomed to having his opinion respected and honoured by his adoring fans; and until this very moment, Florencia would have counted herself among them. What had changed? When had she become cynical? When had she started to question his ideas? She knew exactly what Father would say; it had begun when she started reading Miss Dexington's writings on the potential for women in society. They'd given her lofty dreams of independence and she'd started to wonder if everything she'd taught was true.

"Quite obviously both. I have nothing further to offer

you. You may leave now. Florencia, please escort our visitor out of the house."

Miss Dexington stood up. "I can make my own way out. It is a negative mark against your character that you will leave the fate of Mr Peyton to me. Good day, Mr Waulker."

Florencia followed her out of the room and waited until the door closed before she returned to Father to confirm their visitor was gone.

"Florencia. I want you to become Miss Dexington's friend. I need to understand more about her and about what she intends to do with Mr Peyton. She is right in one aspect; it would be a terrible look for the Luddite cause and those who believe in us to see us abandon Mr Peyton. Our supporters need to know that we will support them."

"Should you write a letter to the papers to get ahead of the Dexington story? Surely they will be discussing the matter with the press too."

"Yes, but I require time to think on what to write. Run along. Make a new friend." Father waved his hand and dismissed her without any thought to exactly how she might achieve the task given his rudeness to her. An apology didn't seem like it would be enough; she'd have to be honest about her own choices to rat out her Father. By the time she'd stepped onto the street, Miss Dexington was long gone, presumably taken away in the hansom cab to her lavish home. Florencia went back inside to get her hat and coat.

"Father. I am just grabbing a few things and will be gone for an hour or so."

"I don't mind how long you spend with our enemy as

long as you bring home useful information. While you are out, please take a message to my physician. I'd like to see him today, if possible."

She rushed into the lounge. "Are you ill?" If he was sick, she couldn't possibly leave him alone.

"Just summon him. Please." Father scowled at the wall, and when she checked his forehead for his temperature—thankfully nice and cool—he growled under his breath.

"Yes Father. I will go now."

# CHAPTER FIVE

After delivering Father's message to his physician, Dr Blake, she went to Miss Dexington's house only to be informed that she was at her office. To have permission to spend time with Miss Dexington seemed unbelievable, except she wasn't tasked with an honest friendship. She was to be a spy and her loyalty to Father, which was already questionable, would come under more scrutiny. Father gave her a safe roof over her head, he cared for her, and she shouldn't feel torn between him and Miss Dexington who she barely knew beyond the opinions she wrote for The Manchester Gentlewoman.

"Miss Dexington." By the time she was ushered into Miss Dexington's office, she probably looked like a harridan having spent an hour walking the hot summer streets of Manchester.

"Miss Waulker. Is there a problem?"

"Father wishes me to become your friend." Florencia blurted out the truth. Instinct told her not to lie to Miss

Dexington; and besides truthful descriptions of the world were her best skill.

"I see. Does he know you've already met me twice previously?"

"No. I shouldn't have done that." She was responsible for this whole sorry mess. If she hadn't gone to warn Miss Dexington, Father would never have been connected with Mr Peyton. Yes, Miss Dexington had told Father that she hadn't found him because of her, but she didn't believe that. She was the connection between Mr Peyton and Father and she'd willingly stood in Miss Dexington's presence and talked about the plot.

"Do you regret making my acquaintance?"

Florencia breathed in sharply. "No, I have absolutely no regrets about that."

"But you do regret something?"

"Yes." She looked around Miss Dexington's office, at the huge mahogany desk and neat piles of papers and shelves of files. "I regret lying to Father about my whereabouts. I didn't need to warn you about Mr Peyton."

"You did... need to warn me, that is."

"But he told you about Father anyway."

Miss Dexington sent her a polite smile, one that conveyed no emotion. "Only because I asked."

"About me?" Florencia pressed her palm against her breastbone. If only the pressure would slow the unsteady thud of her heart.

"No. I didn't want to place you in an awkward position, and it's the first rule of these type of engagements. Always protect the source." Miss Dexington made Florencia feel like a spy, a liar who cheated both sides of a relationship for her own gain. She wanted to shed her skin and wash herself clean. "I asked him why his sudden arrival in Manchester coincided with rumours of a bombing, rumours that came directly from the humble walker's writings."

"And he just told you who Father was?" That fiend was probably trying to get himself out of trouble.

"Have some faith in those who believe in your Father's cause. I read the papers like everyone else. It didn't take much work to put a timeline together with the humble walker's writings, Mr Peyton's arrival, and your comment about the bombing." It was obvious Miss Dexington was attempting to ease Florencia's feelings, but she felt no relief that her story had been corroborated like that.

"It took some diligence to marry up his stories with different sources, one of which led us to your Father as a potential candidate for the source of the humble walker's writings. When I learned that Mr Waulker had an adopted daughter, one Florencia Waulker of Chinese descent, I made the connection myself and decided to call on you."

"I suppose there are not many other Miss Waulker's with my heritage."

"No. Although the spelling of your name did send me down a few dead ends."

"It derives from workers who walked on wool to help bind it into cloth."

Miss Dexington smiled. "Please have a seat. If we are to be friends, we should start on the right footing."

"You don't mind?"

"That a beautiful intelligent young woman with a complex problem wishes to be my friend? No."

"But I'm here to spy on your family."

"You are the most honest spy I've ever encountered."

Florencia blinked at the surreal notion. "Leaving aside the interesting notion that I'm not the first spy you've met, what do you mean?"

"I mean that your Father is a forthright character and you showed incredible bravery to go against his wishes and warn me of Mr Peyton's plans to bomb the factory. I understand feeling torn between being seen to do the right thing and wanting to follow one's heart."

"Whatever do you mean?"

"May I call you Florencia? You may call me Elspeth."

"Elspeth." The name rolled off her tongue easily and she could easily hear herself whisper it roughly against Elspeth's skin late at night. A flush of heat prickled her cheeks.

"Are you feeling well?" Miss Dexington—Elspeth—asked.

"Yes. It's just... It's not right that you welcome my friendship knowing what I've done and what I plan to do."

"On the contrary. It would make me the worst type of scoundrel to send you packing whilst knowing your Father expects you to be my friend."

"But well within your rights to do so." Florencia blushed. Elspeth's insistence they be friends with the most obvious lack of logic in her reasoning might just mean she felt the same flickering chemistry. Now who was being ridiculous.

Florencia cleared her throat. "What precisely is your plan here?"

"You are assuming I have a plan, a deliberate action to deal with this whole situation." Elspeth waved her hand.

"I've read all your writings, so yes, I assumed you have a plan. Why be my friend, if not for some wider scheme?"

Elspeth smiled. "Why not simply want to be your friend?"

"I wish I could trust in such simplicity." More than that, she wished she could trust her own motivations. She'd already defied Father to warn Elspeth because of a potentially misplaced admiration for her. What would happen if she had to choose between the two?

"Are we going to outline our wishes? I wish for a friend who doesn't see the fancy Miss Dexington, but who merely sees Elspeth."

"I am not that person. I cannot be, not with Father's request swirling between us."

"Oh bosh to that. I feel you have been honest with me. We can figure out a satisfaction."

Florencia didn't know what to make of Miss Dexington. Elspeth. This entire conversation was utterly confusing. "You want to be my friend?"

"Yes, my dear. And I believe you need a friend."

Florencia closed her eyes. Was she so transparent? "I have friends." If one counted their cook and their maid.

"A person can't have too many friends."

"Friendship is a luxury that requires time to thrive." Florencia didn't have time. Even now, she'd been away from home for an hour. Father would need her to write out his latest letters.

"What a wise statement, my friend. That must be one of the reasons why I struggle to make friends."

The admission had Florencia staring at Elspeth. "I don't need your sympathy or the way to ignore the truth of our meeting. I'm sure someone in your position in life has many friends."

"There are many who wish to call themselves my friend, yes. As to true friends, it is difficult to find people who overlook my family's fortune and see the real me."

"How do you know I'm not doing exactly that? I approached you with the full knowledge of your connections."

Elspeth shrugged one shoulder. "Your continual doubt is proof enough."

"I'll take your word for it. Shall we discuss Mr Peyton?" Florencia changed the subject, tired of going in circles on a topic that was beyond her experience. She doubted her own motives with regards to her initial decision to warn Elspeth and every step since, and now Elspeth was confusing her with her odd regard for her friendship.

"Yes. Tell me more about the character of Mr Peyton. He showed no remorse on getting caught and taken to the local magistrate for questioning."

Florencia took a moment to gather her thoughts. "He's a firecracker of a person, more extreme than Father in his beliefs."

"Do elaborate."

"He believes that the machines must be stopped, and artisan workers protected so their skills are not lost to history. No method is too extreme. The Lords who make the laws will only pay attention with violent acts; that's what he says." Florencia shuddered. Father only wanted to develop trade unions for the workers; Mr Peyton wanted to bring down the government completely.

"He makes you uncomfortable?"

"Yes." Florencia didn't want to elaborate on the way Mr Peyton stared with crawling possessive gaze that made her shudder. Mr Peyton knew Father couldn't see and he looked at her as though he fully intended to take advantage of the fact. "Father is content to write letters and draw attention to change. I know he was rude to you, but he is fair in his dealings with the issues. He wants to help people."

"You must have felt very strongly to defy your Father and speak to me."

"I was worried about Mr Peyton. He's a... a force of nature and Father's reasoning couldn't stop him."

"Mr Waulker didn't want the bombing to happen?"

Florencia shook her head. It wasn't that simple; Father didn't exactly condone the bombing, but he had done nothing to stop it either. Some readers might interpret his writings as encouraging or inciting violence and she always insisted he was cautious when he dictated those portions. On occasion, he listened. "You've read his letters. You know his mind as much as I do."

"That is no answer at all. Perhaps you are well suited to

this spying business." Elspeth smiled, leaving Florencia uncertain about whether she meant it or not.

"There are two schools of thought among those in the Luddite movement. Either people want to use the anger people felt at Burton's militia shooting into the crowd to grow resentment against the manufacturing businesses; or they want to slow down and ensure that no one else gets hurt."

"And Mr Peyton? Where is he?"

"The former with the added bonus of wanting to go further. Fight harder. Make more noise and mess until the business owners capitulate to his requirements."

"He wants to hold businesses to ransom for their own safety?"

Florencia's mouth dried. "I suppose you could say it that way. He wants the world to pay attention, and with the first Luddite gaining such traction over the physical smashing of a machine, he believes that is the best methodology."

"I take it you disagree."

"Outright war never solved anything. People, innocent people, have already been hurt and I agree with Father that the march of machinery can't be stopped. We need to adjust and redress the balance between worker and factory owner."

"It is about more than that; the production of more affordable cloth allows more people to purchase it. Cheaper clothing means everyone can afford new clothes, not hand-me-downs and turned cuffs."

Florencia hadn't considered that aspect of the matter. "Says the manufacturer. If more accessible clothing comes with children working long hours, falling asleep under machines, and losing fingers, then it's not worth it. You think in profit and how you can increase your sales, but not about the people who make this all possible."

"The Dexington factories have the best safety record in Manchester."

Florencia had heard this argument before. It was one Father had written about many times. "A record that means absolutely nothing when the bar is so low. How many children lost a finger this year in your factories? This week? How many adults have cotton lungs?"

"We do not manufacture with cotton."

Florencia jerked in surprise at Elspeth's harsh retort. "Excuse me?"

"We manufacture wool, linen, and silk. Cotton has the business advantage of being much cheaper as a source material, however, there is no ethical source of cotton, and thus far, the Dexington factories do not handle cotton."

"Are you referring to Wilberforce's law?" The 1807 Slave Trade Act prohibited British ships from engaging in trading of slaves and had caused considerable debate in the papers. People still debated whether the law went far enough.

"The law is only the first step." Elspeth's agreement with Florencia's thought aligned with her refusal to use cotton in the Dexington factories. "People are still being used in those roles across the globe, and many of them are treated in the most horrific ways to produce cotton. I refuse to be associated with slavery, or indentured labour, in any way shape or form. I know that's an unfashionable view among my peers, many of whom have made incredible profits from trading in cotton and sugar."

"It surprises me that you can draw a line like that so readily."

"Why is it a surprise? Humans should not be bought and sold like chattel. People must have choice."

Florencia sighed. "Of course people must have a choice. Is it a choice to begin work as a child, rather than learn your letters? Is it a choice to work long hours operating a dangerous machine simply so one can feed their family?"

"Those people are getting paid and they are free to change jobs at any point they wish. They are not the property of anyone but themselves."

Florencia nodded. She regretted her question as it made her sound ignorant of the plight of those stolen from their homelands and forced into slavery. "Yes. I agree there is a vast difference between having no choice and a small choice. I only wanted to point out that some choices are not simple matters."

"And yet, those who work in our factories still have choices over their own lives. Even the tiniest choice, one that is hard fought where the options are all difficult, elevates someone above the horrors of being forced into slavery."

Florencia nodded again. "You are right. I was wrong to try and draw a comparison between the two. Please accept my apology for my ignorance." What a foolish notion to believe she could argue with Elspeth; of course there was no comparison between the factory workers and slaves, and she really ought not to have started such a line of thinking. She'd read many terrible accounts on the evils of slavery to know better.

"I am but one woman, Florencia Waulker. I cannot change the world. I cannot vote, nor own property of my own. But I will fight damned hard to ensure the Dexington name is not sullied by a connection to the cotton trade."

Florencia smiled slowly. "I would be honoured to be your friend, Elspeth Dexington. Let's work together to improve working conditions in the factories for all, and prevent the use of violence." She wasn't going to completely roll over and accept Elspeth's dismissal of her point just because she had a similarly strong viewpoint on a different matter.

Elspeth's face lit up in a great smile and it took Florencia all her willpower to stay in her seat and not do something ridiculous like kiss her.

# CHAPTER SIX

E lspeth stopped wanting to throttle Florencia for parroting her Father's writing, but that swiftly turned into wanting to kiss her as she bravely apologised. Her brother Humphrey may not have done anything with her letter summoning him to assist her in her fight to stop her own father investing in cotton, but it didn't matter anymore. She had a supporter on her side. The notion made her smile disappear and she scoffed. "Of course, what two women may achieve is only marginally more than what one may do."

"Virtually nothing." Florencia laughed, and the bitter note in the air matched the bitterness on Elspeth's tongue. The reality of their situation, of their station and the way the law viewed them meant that their only power was to subtly convince the men in their lives that their ideas were their own and thus must be acted upon, and not planted there by women.

"I must go home to Father. What should I tell him?"

"Mr Peyton is in the custody of Sir Adamson, the local magistrate. He hasn't learned to hold his tongue, so a visit might be in order if your Father wishes to know what Mr Peyton has been saying, or perhaps your Father enjoys listening to Mr Peyton and would visit for that reason alone." She stood up and walked around her desk towards Florencia. With one hand held out, she offered Florencia a help upwards. Florencia placed her hand in Elspeth's palm and warmth rushed up her arm with such pace as outstripped a galloping horse. She almost jerked away, having never felt such a physical connection before. Of course, she'd kissed other girls before; at school where such things were dismissed as silliness, but nothing like this. Nothing like the shocking rush of desire that had her wanting to pull Florencia closer and never let her go.

"Oh." Florencia's cheeks bloomed with pink. "Do you feel that?" She whispered.

"Yes. I think I might want to be more than your friend." Elspeth whispered in return; her voice strangely rough as she stared at their hands resting together. She brushed her thumb over Florencia's wrist, hopeful, needy. Florencia slowly rose to her feet and stood there. Very close. So close that Elspeth could feel Florencia's breath against her own cheeks, and each inhale included the scent of thyme and the illusive perfume that belonged to Florencia.

"My cook's sister lives with another woman as if they are married. I understand what you are asking, and I think I would like that too." Florencia's forthright description made her spine tingle and her skin flush with heat.

"In that case..." Elspeth pressed a kiss to Florencia's lips. At first hesitant, and then when Florencia responded, the kiss became insistent. Urgent. It was more than lips brushing against each other, it was like she'd found her very essence. Her true match. The world faded to the connection of their kiss. Elspeth's clothes were too tight, and she wanted to run away from her office, dragging Florencia to a private space.

"Oh." She stepped backwards, reluctantly leaving Florencia's warm touch. "We can't do this in my office." Elspeth gulped. Anyone might knock or walk in and see them, and while kisses between wasn't precisely illegal, not like for men, it certainly would result in the biggest scandal and would undermine any influence she might have with her Father.

"I need to get back to Father. He gets frustrated without me to tell him what is happening in the world."

Elspeth squared her shoulders. "We should meet again."

"Yes, please." Florencia's voice had a husky undertone that sent fresh shivers down Elspeth's spine and created a soft wetness between her thighs where she touched herself late at night.

"I would offer my house although I suspect you can't leave your Father for long." Elspeth wished she could invite herself to Florencia's house, however, she suspected it wouldn't be a welcoming place for her; not with her own Father being on the opposite side of the machinery debate to Florencia's father.

"Once a week, Father's physician visits for two hours and I have that time to myself. We could meet at an inn?"

"I would like that very much. Please send me a note and I

will be there." Elspeth wasn't sure how she would wait until then, and when a knock thudded on her office door, she realised that she would have to figure that out.

"Enter."

"Miss Dexington, there is a man here to see you. He didn't identify himself but he said that you would see him once you saw this letter." The man, Mr Smythe, one of their newly employed men from the local militia to protect the factories handed her a piece of paper.

"I will be going then." Florencia picked up her bag and coat and fled before Elspeth had the chance to say anything further. The letter was her own one to Humphrey and all the blood in her head fell to her feet and she had to sit down. If a messenger was bringing her own letter to her, it couldn't be good news. "Please show him in."

Mr Smythe nodded and left, and Elspeth wished she could hold Florencia's hand again. She wasn't sure how long she sat there until Mr Smythe entered again followed by...

"Humphrey."

"Shoosh. Father can't know I'm here."

Elspeth barely heard him and she leaped across the room and wrapped her arms around her brother. She hadn't seen him for years. "How are you?"

"I'm excellent. It's very strange to be here after so long and to see you like this. With your own office. Well done, darling sister."

"The office is nothing without the ability to influence Father's bad decisions."

Humphrey stepped back from their hug, his hands resting

on her shoulders. "I'm not sure how you think I will influence him either. He banished me from the family."

"He will have seen sense by now. It's been years and you are his only son."

Humphrey shook his head. "No. I am still the same person that he threw away. And more than that, he banished me for a youthful affair. Once he discovers the truth—well, never mind that, I can hardly talk about that without risking my own life..." Humphrey's gulp had Elspeth pulling him right back into a hug.

"I understand, more than you could imagine. I should not have asked you for this."

Humphrey tilted his head, considering her. "You?"

"It is early days for myself and ..." She stopped herself mid-whisper before mentioned Florencia's name, not only because these things weren't safe to talk about aloud, but also because one spectacular kiss didn't make a relationship.

"Is Father causing an issue?"

Elspeth laughed. "He doesn't know. The issue I mentioned in the letter is one of business. I had hoped you might assist me in changing his mind on a very serious matter."

Humphrey shook his head sadly. "I very much doubt that he would give me an audience, and to expect him to listen to my opinion is unfortunately going to result in him doing the opposite of what I ask of him."

"You could tell him that an investment in cotton is great. People overlook the dreadful source of the fabric in favour of cheaper clothing." The words tasted wrong on her tongue and she shook her head. "No, scratch that. If you said that, he'd probably think you'd finally grown up to agree with his perspective. Please don't encourage him."

Humphrey laughed. "I may have many influences across the government through my work with Mr Mattson, however, I have no ability to change Father's mind on anything. I do have one important question for you, however."

"Yes?"

"If he finds out about you, do you have funds to leave? Do you have a safe space? I have some funds set aside, and will set you up in a household if you require. You've always been my favourite sister."

Elspeth shoved her brother on the shoulder. "Bosh to the idea of favourites. You love all of us. And no, you don't need to worry about me. I will be fine without Father's money." She had her own five percent fund that she'd been adding to over the years. A rainy day fund because she knew her position was precarious. A spinster who never wished to have a husband needed to plan for her future, and she'd known that since her first blush of womanhood.

"Come on, Humphrey. Let's go and eat together and figure out a plan. The Horse and Hops Inn does an excellent beef pie." Elspeth wrapped her pelisse around her shoulders and walked out of her office with a nod to Smythe as she passed him in the corridor. "Mr Smythe. I will return in a couple of hours. I am not expecting any messages, however, if there is anything urgent we will be at the Horse and Hops."

"Do I need to accompany you?"

"No. You need to stay here and keep this place safe from another of Mr Peyton's men. Thank you."

Mr Smythe stared at Humphrey over her shoulder and she realised the issue. She'd employed Mr Smythe to be protective and he was only doing his job.

"I'm sorry. Please meet my brother Mr Dexington. I realise this introduction places you in a difficult situation, but I need some time to talk to my brother without the elder Mr Dexington knowing he is in town. There is a complex family situation that I'm trying to negotiate. Forgive me for not introducing my brother and easing your concerns about my safety. Thank you for doing your job well, Mr Smythe." Perhaps she laid it on a little thick, like expensive whitewash, but from the way he nodded with a little colour across his cheeks, she knew her words had done the trick. It was only after they left the office and Humphrey walked beside her that he elbowed her gently and grinned.

"I see I'm not the only one blessed with the Dexington charm."

"Shush. Come and eat and tell me everything that you've been doing." She almost skipped giddily beside her brother, thrilled to see him after so many apart. In the quiet of the Horse and Hops, she could tell him all about Florencia and hear all about his life and hopes and dreams. Just like old times. Just like in their letters but without the vague hints they needed to use as protection from the law, on the off chance that someone else might read their private correspondence.

# CHAPTER SEVEN

Nothing reminded Florencia of the vast gulf between her life and Elspeth's more than to hear someone walk into her office with an introduction. Elspeth belonged to a wealthy family who owned several factories in Manchester. Even without being a member of the aristocracy, Elspeth had enough money to buy anything she required. Florencia's life, by contrast, was a lot more fragile. Without Father she had no income, no roof over her head, and no means to change that. She left, quickly, in the fashion of a bolting horse fleeing an unexpected gust of wind, and rushed home. Her life with Father might be constrictive and often frustrating, but she was needed by him and he gave her safety. That had to matter. Didn't it?

How had one kiss upended the way she viewed her whole life? It couldn't happen again. It must have been an accident. Florencia's chest tightened. What was she about? People didn't accidentally kiss someone. She pressed her fingers against her lips, remembering the sensation and taste of Elspeth. The burning in her chest continued and she shook out her hands. She needed to forget the kiss—impossible—and get back to her life, so she burst through the front door and stormed into the lounge. Her legs came to a screaming halt and she rubbed her eyes. Father was kissing the physician? Or more accurately, Dr Blake was seated in Father's lap, kissing him.

"I'm so sorry. I will leave."

"No, child. It is fine. Please sit down." Dr Blake moved rapidly to stand beside Father, and if it wasn't for the way his hand rested on Father's shoulder, she might have wondered if she'd imagined what she'd seen.

"I don't mind. I understand." Well, perhaps not the tender relationship between Father and the physician, but she definitely understood the desire for something outside the bounds of society. She wanted more kisses with Elspeth, and she had a million questions for Father. If she felt such desires, was she broken like people said? A sinner like the religious writings in the papers? Or was this real and is so, why did society want to stop them? And if what she felt was real, how could she know if Elspeth was the one? Or just the first person who understood her and wanted her?

"Please sit down." Dr Blake had such a strong tone in his voice that she sat without thought.

"Father." Habit broke through her surprise. "My expression is one of acceptance and confusion. I didn't expect this. I'm surprised that's all."

"She is correct in her description." Dr Blake's fingers tightened on Father's shoulder.

"Florencia." Father's calm voice helped slow her heart. She knew all his tones and this one soothed her the most. "My dear daughter. There is something you need to understand about me, and it's incredibly important that you keep this secret."

"I know the law, Father. I would never endanger you."

"Thank you. Dr Blake, George, is the love of my life. I would sacrifice everything for him."

Florencia knew this was her moment to be brave. "If that is true, then I also would sacrifice everything for him." And she hoped they would both do the same for her, if it ever came to be. The intake of breath rang in the room, a loud indication of surprise. She swallowed.

"You didn't expect me to stay?"

"No, my dear girl. Florencia. It is dangerous to love like this. I don't expect you to take that risk."

Something caught in her throat, like a sob and a laugh. "Every day I risk you being sent to jail with the letters you write. Sedition is as serious a charge as this one."

"Clever girl. And yet with your help, we always manage to stay within the lines of the law thanks to your advice."

"And we will do the same again, won't we?" Dr Blake said. His authoritative tone echoed in the room.

"Do you doubt me?" Florencia had never met Dr Blake before, and all she knew of him was the weekly appointment he had with Father. Oh. Oooohh. She blinked and tried not to let her shock show. They must have been having this relationship for years under the guise of Dr Blake's visits to check on Father's health. The cleverness of the scheme made her want to smile, but the smile disappeared just as fast as she realised the real meaning of this. They loved each other. Deeply, by the way Dr Blake stared at Father, and all they could have was a couple of hours a week.

"I have absolute faith in my daughter, George. She will protect us, just as she has been a loyal companion to me all these years." Father paused for a second. "How is Miss Dexington?" There was a touch of humour in his tone, a change that gave her pause. Well... this was interesting.

"Did you plan for her to find you? She made the connection between Mr Peyton and your writings easily enough."

"Florencia, I have listened to you read the papers to me twice a day for more than twenty years..."

"Twenty-three." She'd been adopted at the age of five, or so the workhouse had said, and she'd been here for twenty-three years since.

"Whenever you read Miss Dexington's writings, I heard a subtle change in your voice and I wondered what that might mean. When I heard a rumour—thank you George—that your Miss Dexington was a considered spinster with connections to a certain women's group rumoured to have certain tendencies, I thought it might be nice for the two of you to meet." Father had deliberately set out to introduce her to Elspeth?

"And you think this is a gift? Or is it a way to keep my silence on your own matter?"

Father grinned. "Ah, my dear, your cynical outlook is a

grand credit to me. Yes, I rather hoped Miss Dexington would be a gift. You adore her writings, and you've never shown any interest in men. So I added a few things together..."

"And came up with twelve? Father." She shouldn't be surprised that he'd known. For someone with no vision, he'd always seen too much. There should be a word for someone like him; someone with superior understanding of human nature. She chuckled and a warm well of happiness bubbled in her chest.

"I had no idea about this." Dr Blake said.

"My darling. You would never have approved." Father laughed and it didn't take long for Dr Blake to join him. He bent down and kissed Father on the cheek.

"In a different world, I would have been here with you all the time and seen your scheming."

"And put a stop to it. You've always been too conservative in your risk taking, George."

"I have needed to be."

Father reached up to hold Dr Blake's hand. "I know. You are the very best of men."

"I will take my leave now." Florencia needed to leave before the happy banter between them and the love shimmering in the air became too stifling. Could she ever have that for herself? And at what cost? They obviously loved each other and yet had to be content with only a couple of hours together alone each week under the guise of Dr Blake's role as Father's physician.

"Before you go, please tell Miss Dexington she is most

welcome in our house at any time." Father had the same sly smile he used when he'd dictated a particularly clever piece of writing to her.

"As you wish." Florencia left the room as quickly as she'd entered it and ran to her bedroom where she stood for a long time, simply holding her palm against her chest. It felt like her entire life had shifted violently into a space where she could be free to explore herself. Well, at least as free as one could be with the rules of society forever breathing down one's neck. She flung herself on her bed and traced her fingertip over her lips again. Kissing Elspeth had been magical. It'd felt like home. Was it like that for every kiss? Or was it only kissing Elspeth that would make her feel like this? She could hardly go out and test this philosophy by kissing random women. There was one thing she could do, though, so she wriggled under her blankets, even though it were only mid-afternoon. With eyes closed, she summoned up the memory of Elspeth's face, close to hers and she could almost feel the whisper of her breath against her face once more. She pressed her fingers to her lips again, then slowly dragged them down her throat, imagining it were Elspeth's touch, down over her rough dress. It was easy to push the fabric aside and touch herself there, where she was slick and wet with wanting. Many times, she'd done this, although never before with the knowledge of a real kiss still making her lips tingle. Every stroke, every press of her fingers, had her squirming, with the delicious tension building. And this time, more than any other time, the moment of release came faster, harder, as she used both hands. Fingers to fill herself and pump, with her other hand rubbing hard on the nerves at the top of her feminine place. She bit her lip to stop herself crying out as her back arched under the blanket.

One day—soon—she wanted to do this with Elspeth.

# CHAPTER EIGHT

A week went by and Florencia neither saw nor heard from Elspeth. Luckily she'd been too busy with Father's correspondence to have too much time to contemplate what the lack of contact meant. After the sensation of Mr Peyton's arrest was published by one of the local papers, everyone had an opinion. The people who mattered to Father —the workers—were apparently torn between wanting an end to the violence that targeted them, while the other group felt the need to do more in order to get the rights they deserved. Father wrote as the humble walker with common sense, calling for calm and non-violent ways to get change through working together as a community.

Father wrote as Mr Peyton's fictional brother, reminding people of the way Burton had shot at the crowd and how it meant that the factory owners felt they had the right to a worker's body and had used this to kill them when they spoke up. Father wrote letters from semi-literate workers, from people who worked in the offices of factories, even one letter from an outspoken anonymous wife of a factory owner claiming their factory workers sang as they worked, and therefore the situation wasn't as bad as everyone made out. Writing that one had enraged her; her fingers shaking as she'd tried to write with such detached insincerity for the people weren't really being seen by the fictional housewife. He wrote so many letters from so many points of view that Florencia started to become unsure of what he really believed anymore, except that his strategy was to get the issue dominating the letters to the editor sections of all the papers. He wanted all of Manchester paying attention to the plight of workers and talking about them.

She stood in the kitchen, scrubbing the ink from her hands, using the best soap. Her fingers were cramped and her skin pink and raw and still the ink wouldn't fade.

"Hello." Elspeth stood at the back door, a vision in a pale blue dress with a chirpy bonnet hiding her black hair.

"Hello." Florencia's voice was rough as she lifted her hands from the bucket and dried them on a rough towel. "What brings you here?" After a whole week with no word, but she didn't say that part.

"I rather thought we should talk."

"Oh? About what?"

Elspeth leaned closer and wrapped her hands over the towel, gently drying Florencia's hands. Somehow she made the rough texture of the towel softer. "About how we kissed and then you bolted from my office and I haven't heard from you in a week. I was worried you thought..."

"So was I. When I didn't hear, I mean." Florencia jumped in with a tumble of words.

"What did you think?"

"That it meant nothing." Florencia blinked. "That you didn't write or visit because I'd overstepped and insulted you in some way."

Elspeth squeezed her hands. "I worried about exactly the same thing. You fled from my office as if my touch had burned you and I heard nothing more. I thought I'd done something wrong."

"No." Florencia swallowed. "You were perfect."

"I was? But you didn't write."

Florencia pulled her hands away and hung up the towel on the little railing above the sink. "Neither did you."

Elspeth drew in a deep breath and smiled. "Neither did I. I'm here now and I'd like to know what you are going to do about it."

"Father says you can stay here whenever you want."

Elspeth blinked. "He did?" Her confusion spread all over her face and Florencia couldn't help it. She giggled.

"I have a lot to tell you. Come." She held out her hand and when Elspeth placed her hand against hers a rush of heat sent prickles up her arm. Together they walked the short distance from the kitchen out the back of the house towards Florencia's bedroom. Perhaps it was selfish, but she had to know. She needed to kiss Elspeth again, and she wanted to touch her in the same way she touched herself. After closing the door to her room, she leaned back against the door.

"Tell me." Elspeth lifted Florencia's hand to her lips and

kissed each knuckle. One at a time, and with each brush of her lips, Florencia's mind emptied until she couldn't speak at all.

"Tell you what?"

"Your Father said I could stay. Does he know what that might mean?"

"That we will kiss."

Elspeth smiled. "And maybe more. Maybe we will be intimate or even, hopefully, fall in love."

"Yes." Florencia closed her eyes for a moment, then opened them slowly. "He knows because he also has a forbidden love. He match-made us."

"The clever fellow. But why me? I'm not exactly in his circle, and I doubt he thinks we are on the same page with regards to our politics."

Florencia's cheeks heated and she bit her lip. It wasn't that simple, and the discussion they'd had about cotton reminded Florencia that Elspeth's views weren't so different to hers. They came from a different point of view; the worker vs the owner, but both cared about people and the impact of business on humanity.

"Why me?" A little frown crossed Elspeth's brow. "He wasn't serious about you spying on me, was he?"

"No. It's just... embarrassing."

"Oh?"

"He heard rumours about you. He runs in those circles, so don't worry about it being common knowledge in Manchester society. And then he added that to my own lack of interest in men, and the—" Florencia cleared her throat.

"Um, the way my voice changes when I read him your writings."

Elspeth's frown disappeared, replaced with a grin. Her deep blue eyes sparkled. "How does your voice change?"

Florencia held her breath for a moment until suddenly her breath rushed out quickly. "Don't tease me like that."

"But it makes your voice all husky and soft."

"Husky and soft. That's not real, Elspeth."

Elspeth's smile widened. "Maybe not, but this is." She leaned forward and kissed her directly on the lips. It couldn't be possible and yet it was. The energy from Elspeth's smile infused the kiss with a joie de vivre that burst inside Florencia's lungs like the steam from one of the looms in a Dexington factory. Noisy and vibrant and productive. So many of Father's followers were scared of the machines, of the changes they were bringing to the world. The machines took away the handmade artisanal skill of the past, replacing it with mass production run by less skilled workers. More could be made for less money and by less people. She thought she understood their worries, and now, in this kiss she realised she knew nothing. Change, and the aspiration for improvement, was the best thing about humanity. She wanted to be filled with the urgent need for Elspeth. Her brain had taken one kiss and was spinning into ideas of forever. She wanted to kiss Elspeth for the rest of her days. On a gasp, she pulled back.

"Wait."

"What is the matter?" Elspeth tilted her head to the side, considering. Florencia knew she should be taking her time. She couldn't. Not when all she could see, all that filled her vision were Elspeth's lips. Reddened by their kisses. She wanted to bite her. A flurry of ideas filled her mind. She wanted to take off Elspeth's beautiful fashionable dress and touch her all over.

"Nothing is the matter. I want you." Florencia didn't have the words to describe what she wanted, only that her body felt like it was catching on fire and her clothes were too rough against her skin. She needed to rip them off and cover Elspeth's body with her own.

"Then have me. Ever since I first saw you, I knew I wanted you. If you feel the same way, then I'm already yours." Elspeth pulled her skirts up. Up and up. Until the entire ensemble was pulled over her head and cast away onto a chair. Until Elspeth stood there in her undergarments with stockings and garters over her drawers and her breasts spilling over her long stays. Until Florencia couldn't breathe for the beauty of the sight before her.

"Can you undo my laces?" Elspeth turned around, and Florencia reached out for laces to undo the long stay that went from under her breasts down to her hips. The fashionable undergarment was the reason her dresses hung so well from her figure, while Florencia made do with the much cheaper short stay. It had the added bonus that she could dress herself; and the obvious difference between their station in life gave Florencia pause. She wanted to see Elspeth without fabric, but she didn't want to act as her servant. For today, just this once, she pushed aside doubt because the urge to undress Elspeth was stronger than any other concern. It didn't take long to untie her laces and release Elspeth's body from her stays because they weren't tightly done, only firm enough to provide support without changing Elspeth's shape. The stays dropped to the ground and Elspeth stepped out the stiff garment and turned around. Before Florencia could begin to describe the sight of Elspeth standing in her room, clad only in a chemise, Elspeth's arms were wrapped around her, with her hands searching for how to take off Florencia's gown.

Soon enough, fabric lay scattered on the floor.

"Kiss me again, Florencia." Elspeth caressed her hands up Florencia's bare arms, and gently rested her palms on Florencia's shoulders. Florencia tried to focus on the joy of the moment, but the uncertainty began to creep in and her brain started to race.

"Wait. I have some questions."

Elspeth nodded. She slid her hands back down Florencia's arms and held her hands. "Come and sit here with me." With a gentle tug, she pulled Florencia towards her bed and together they sat on the end of it.

"Um." Florencia wasn't sure where to start.

"Have you ever kissed someone before?" Elspeth's voice was soft and welcoming.

"Only you. Have you?"

"Desire is difficult for people like us. I've only kissed one other girl, back when I was at school. We were very young. It has been years for me as well, because, well... You know all the reasons why. As I age, I get more and more understanding about the risks involved and it's hard to step past that."

Florencia couldn't bring herself to ask Elspeth why she'd

taken that step for her. "I'm glad you kissed me. It's just I have all these questions about the future."

"Like?"

"Is this flutter I feel in my chest when I'm around you real? Is it temporary because kissing you is exciting? Or is it the beginning of love?"

"Love. Bosh to that."

Florencia pulled her hands away and jumped to her feet. "You don't believe in love?"

"No." Elspeth sighed. "I want to, but I can't imagine it's for me."

"So, why are you here?"

"I guess I'm hoping that we can be friends."

"I don't kiss my friends."

"Except me." Elspeth's cheeky grin burned bright, flickering in Florencia's chest. "The future for women is uncertain. We can't own property, we can't vote, the whole world is set up for us to belong to a man, and I know with absolute certainty that I'd make any husband miserable. And to be honest, most women marry for security not love, so what does love mean anyway? People seem to make the best of the life they've been dealt, and I think that's the best I can hope for too."

"What does that mean for us? I know it's early days. We haven't known each other long, and it's far too soon to be discussing our future. I—" Florencia felt incredibly vulnerable; exposed with all her feelings on display. Her lack of clothing only exacerbated the sense of emotional nakedness.

"If I was to be pragmatic, I'm staring at a future where I'll never marry and I would like a friend and a companion to come home to. I see my older sisters, and my brother, all creating homes with their husbands, and I want that. So yes, I don't know yet if that's with you, but I'd really like it to be. Of all the people I've met in my life, you fascinate me. I don't expect love, but I'd love to have companionship."

"And kisses." Florencia could imagine a life where Elspeth came to live with her and Father, and would come home from the Dexington offices every evening to eat dinner with them, discuss the world's issues, and go to bed together later.

"Oh, most definitely kisses." Elspeth tilted her head slightly. "Come here. Let's kiss. The future can wait. I'm here right now and I want you."

Florencia drew in a deep breath and the anxiety over tomorrow began to fade. As Father said, change took time and many small steps. It was time to take the first small step towards a life with Elspeth. Her knees wobbled a little as she walked towards the bed. She stood with her thighs touching Elspeth's dangling legs and pressed against Elspeth's knees until she spread them enough for Florencia to stand between.

# CHAPTER NINE

Elspeth pressed her knees against the outside of Florencia's thighs. For all her bold talking, she was barely more experienced than Florencia. This—being almost naked with another woman—was new to her too. A few experimental kisses at school hadn't prepared her for this moment. Her own heart thudded quickly in her chest and her breathing became shallow. All she had was the knowledge of her own body; and she sent up a quick thank you to her older sisters who had spoken openly about the marriage bed.

"What's the matter?" Florencia cupped her cheek with a soft hand.

Elspeth shook her head. "Aren't we a pair? I'm nervous."

"But you've done this before?"

"I've kissed before. I've never—" Elspeth paused, her face burning hot.

"Oh. Perhaps we should get under the sheets and just

cuddle?" Florencia's solution sounded perfect, and Elspeth giggled.

"Perhaps we should. After all, why rush? We have our whole lifetime to figure this out."

Florencia's hand tightened against her face. "We do?"

"I reckon we do. I don't know about you, but I want to spend more time with you. Not just here in bed, but as your friend. I think I really need a friend." Bosh; now she was babbling.

"Get under the covers, Elspeth. I want to kiss you and touch you and I'm nervous too. We shouldn't just stand here, getting cold and talking ourselves out of something we both want." Florencia's commanding tone reminded Elspeth of some of her Father's letters. She wriggled backwards on the bed until her back hit the bedhead, then tucked herself under the blankets as requested. The bed swayed as Florencia clambered in the side. Her weight shifted the tiny mattress and they rolled together into the middle of the bed. They both shrieked at the shock of their bodies touching, then giggled.

"Oh boy, you make me feel like a giddy school girl again." Elspeth was too old for that feeling, but there was something so lovely about being under a blanket with Florencia that she wanted to burst with happiness.

"I've never been that person. I had a governess when I was young—"

"A governess?"

Florencia rolled her eyes. "I know. We aren't exactly rich, but Father adopted me so I could write for him, so he invested in a governess to teach me to write. She used to write his letters, and I would copy them until I was good enough to do it myself." There was something fleeting in Florencia's tone that made Elspeth curious.

"What aren't you telling me?"

Florencia sighed. "It wasn't one governess. Each one only lasted a year or two; they couldn't cope with Father's endless need to write. Looking back it wasn't much of a job for a young woman, and whenever they'd get a proposal of marriage, they would leave."

"Leaving you alone again." Elspeth assumed the governesses had taken on the motherly role for a young Florencia.

"After a while it didn't matter anymore, and then I learned to be self-sufficient. It's only been Father and I for a while now." Florencia kissed Elspeth on the forehead. "And he gets the physician for two hours once a week, but enough about me." Florencia let her mouth drift down over Elspeth's face, until they were kissing properly, and all conversation could wait until later.

"This feels so subversive." Elspeth whispered as she nibbled and kissed down Florencia's throat.

Florencia giggled as she slid her hands under Elspeth's chemise. "It is. We aren't supposed to be happy."

"Or find pleasure outside of the restrictions of marriage." Elspeth nuzzled against Florencia's small breasts, and Florencia gasped as Elspeth licked her hard nubbins.

"Oh. Do that again." Florencia stroked her hands all over Elspeth's skin, loving the softness under her palms, and grateful that her version of manual labour was mostly writing, so her fingertips were also soft with her only callouses being from her pen. As they explored, fabric got in the way and they giggled softly against each other's skin, discovering what each other liked. Florencia loved it all; she'd never imagined her body could feel like this, so connected to someone else, so alive and flammable, filled with heat and passion. When Elspeth slid her hand between Florencia's legs, she wanted to do the same to Elspeth.

"Can I?"

"Yes. Have you touched yourself there before?" Elspeth's whisper made gooseflesh rise across her skin.

"Yes. I like it here." She moved Elspeth's fingers to the sensitive place at the top of her folds and showed Elspeth how she liked to touch herself.

"Fascinating. I do it slightly differently." Elspeth took Florencia's fingers and guided them in a circular motion, rubbing firmly until Elspeth squirmed and moaned. Elspeth released her hand to focus on giving Florencia the same attention, and together they delighted each other, until Florencia had no choice but to kiss Elspeth and drink in her breathy cries. They came together; with Florencia's blood rushing in her ears and heat surging inside her as if she'd fallen from a galloping horse but never to hit the ground, just to fly and fly until she landed on a soft cloud with a deep sigh from far inside herself.

"Elspeth."

"Florencia."

They lay there together, holding each other, with the blankets in disarray and Florencia's heart was tender. After a long time, Elspeth chuckled.

"I can see why men want to keep us ignorant of any possibility that doesn't include them. It must scare them to know that there are a few women in the world who don't need them and can find this without them."

"I think they are more bothered by anything that interrupts their sense of superiority. Look at my father and his physician. Society would condemn their love because it threatens the need for dominance in a family and in the world."

"I see. It's not about all men, but about anyone who dares to life a live that doesn't conform to the life that allows the men in charge to stay in charge."

Florencia smiled. "Poor fragile creatures who own the world. Having everything isn't enough; they also need to stop anyone from having anything they don't approve of."

"And all the while, most people aspire to be them."

Florencia bit her bottom lip. She wouldn't exactly put it that way. "Not necessarily. Most people aspire to a life well-lived. They aspire to safe working conditions, so they can come home to their loved ones. They aspire to being paid enough to pay their bills with a little left over for fun. People are allowed fun."

Elspeth frowned. "You are your father's daughter."

"You disagree?"

"No. I think I need to spend more time in contemplation

of my assumptions about people. I've grown up as a factory owner's daughter with all the privilege that comes with that, and yes, all the ego associated with feeling superior simply due to the luck of my upbringing."

Florencia sighed with satisfaction. Physical pleasure was one thing, but this—this meeting of minds and challenging each other other's perceptions of the world—was even better. "Let's learn together."

"And change the world together."

It might be foolish infatuation, but Florencia suddenly envisioned a life together, writing to the newssheets, inspiring other people to think about how to make the world a better place for the majority. It would truly be a life's work, or more likely the work of several lifetimes. But she felt hope grow in her chest because she'd found someone to do the work with her and supporting her.

# EPILOGUE

JUNE 1814

"Darling Elspeth. Did you know it has been two years since we first met?" Florencia stood in the kitchen, packing fresh bread, some cheese, and a bottle of Bourdeaux sherry. Today she planned to celebrate their first meeting with a picnic on the back lawn of their new house. On their anniversary last year, Elspeth had taken her to a brand new house, built for specifically for them with rooms for Father. Father's rooms were an exact replica of the rooms he used in their old cottage, so it was easy for him to navigate around them, and over the last year, he'd slowly learned the rest of their new house. The house was on the outskirts of Manchester, situated on the Bridgewater canal. The lawn behind the house had a large oak tree and today she planned to spread out a blanket and celebrate with Elspeth in the summer sun.

"Yes. And I've been looking forward to this picnic ever since you wrote it on the calendar two weeks ago." Elspeth's charming grin thrilled Florencia and she abandoned her packing to kiss her.

"I love you."

"And I love you. Remember our first time. Bosh, we were so nervous." Florencia still couldn't believe her luck in getting to love Elspeth.

"And it was wonderful."

"Every day since, it's been wonderful to come home to you and cuddle you at night."

"I like having a home for you to come to. We might never be allowed to marry, and we are unlikely to have children—" Florencia let her words fade away.

"Don't say that. If you truly want a child, we can adopt one. It worked for your Father. Why shouldn't it work for us?"

"A lonely little girl who loves to read. Yes, I think I would like that." Florencia already had the gift of love from Father, and from Elspeth, and now she could imagine loving a group of children too.

"You would be an excellent mother."

Florencia nodded. "I rather think that is true. Now, come, let's enjoy the summer sunshine and a bottle of wine to celebrate two wonderful years."

"And tomorrow, I will take you to the workhouse and we can choose our new family."

Florencia jabbed Elspeth in the ribs. "Stop making it

sound so mercenary. You know I'll find it impossible to leave anyone behind."

Elspeth sighed. "I'm sorry." She kissed Florencia, a lover's kiss on the mouth, and it was long time before Florencia could speak.

"I do wish we could take them all." Elspeth showed her understanding. Over the past two years, she'd changed the working conditions at the Dexington factories to improve safety and under Florencia's guidance every worker had to spend a couple of hours a week learning to read. Coincidentally, those two hours occurred while George, the physician, came to visit Father for his weekly check-up, and it was an unspoken agreement between them that Florencia would leave the house to give him the space he needed with his lover.

"It's an impossible decision."

"It is, but I believe in you. You'll make the right decision."

"Thank you. Now, come along, let's eat." Florencia's heart was in her mouth as she picked up the basket and led Elspeth out into the sunshine. Two women might not be able to change all the unfairness in the world, but they could make a good life for a few people, and teach their children how to keep improving the world. After all, it would be the work of several lifetimes to get the vote for women and ensure equality under law. For now, any small gains would have to be enough. Together they could live and love and do their best.

If you enjoyed this book, and you want more sapphic historical romance, you'll love my GREAT WAR series beginning with HER LADY'S MELODY.

*An aristocrat hiding from her past, a doctor hiding from her grief, a journey that will be a danger to themselves... and their hearts!*

War doctor Luciana Stanmore was not healed by the singing of the armistice last year. Unable to face returning to England without the lover the war took from her, she goes instead to seek comfort with her grandmother in Amsterdam, where the beautiful widow next door catches her eye.

If anyone discovers Therese de Seletsky's identity, it would be all over for her Russian aristocrat son. She lost her husband to the Bolsheviks and she'll do anything to keep Pavel safe, including denying her own need for music and love. When he breaks his arm playing, Therese risks accepting the help of her mysterious new neighbour, and ignores the tug of attraction between them.

An attempted kidnap of Pavel changes everything. Therese can only turn to Luciana, and England, to unlock the secret of why she's being targeted. Along the way, they draw closer, but how can they love when the pain of the past is a present threat?

A steamy girl next door lesbian story of yearning, hope, and new love after loss. HEA guaranteed.

# ACKNOWLEDGMENTS

I pay my respects to the Wangal people of the Eora Nation, who are the traditional owners of the land on which this book was written.

Thank you to Lina, the Word Makers, the Carina discord, and Ebony's anthology groups. You've all championed this series and your support has kept me writing during a difficult year in my personal life.

# AUTHOR NOTES

The common English surname Walker derives from Waulker and is an occupational name for someone whose job was literally to 'walk' over cloth after weaving wool to clean and thicken it. The job was also known as 'fulling'.

In Roman society, slaves walked on the cloth while ankle deep in tubs of human urine, as the urine provided ammonium salts which cleansed and whitened the cloth.

In the Scottish Gaelic tradition, fulling or waulking was done by pounding the woollen cloth with a club or the walker's feet. The job was traditionally done by women who sang waulking songs to set the pace.

From the medieval period onwards, this process underwent the innovation of having the cloth stretched on frames known as tenters (attached with tenterhooks), and then a watermill drove a series of hammers to beat the cloth. This process caused the woollen fibres to 'felt' together which gave it strength and increased waterproofing.

In April 1812, eight Luddites were killed when soldiers fired into a crowd of 2,000 protestors near Manchester. The English Prime Minister Spencer Perceval was assassinated in May 1812.

# ALL BOOKS BY RENÉE DAHLIA

Thanks for reading THE SECRET LIFE OF SPINSTERS. I hope you enjoyed it.

Reviews can help readers find books, and I am grateful for all honest reviews. Thank you for taking the time to let others know what you've read, and what you thought.

If you write a review for THE SECRET LIFE OF SPINSTERS and email me I will send you a free copy of any of my other books of your choice. My email is renee@reneedahlia.com.

If you'd like to know more about me, my books, or to connect with me online, you can visit my webpage

www.reneedahlia.com

and if you sign up to my newsletter, you can grab a free book.

Twitter https://twitter.com/dekabat
Facebook https://www.facebook.com/reneedahliawriter/
Instagram https://www.instagram.com/reneedahlia_author/
Patreon https://www.patreon.com/reneedahlia
BookBub https://www.bookbub.com/authors/renee-dahlia

*Historical Series: Desiring the Dexingtons*

1. Love Wasn't Built in a Day (mm)
2. The Secret Life of Spinsters (ff)
3. The Widow's Modiste (ff)

*Historical Series: Great War*

1. Her Lady's Melody (ff)
2. Her Lady's Fortune (ff)
3. Her Lady's Honor (ff)
4. His Lord's Soldier (mm)

*Historical Series: Bluestockings*

Prequel: The Shipwrecked Earl's Bride (fm with bisexual hero)

1. To Charm a Bluestocking (fm with bisexual hero)
2. In Pursuit of a Bluestocking (fm)
3. The Heart of a Bluestocking (fm)

*Contemporary Series: Gamble Racing*

1. Driven to Distraction (mm)
2. Driven by Passion (mm)
3. Driven by Ambition (mm)
4. Driven to Protect (mm)

*Contemporary Series: Seraph's Burlesque Club*

1. Show Up (ff with bisexual heroine)
2. Show Off (ff with bisexual heroines)
3. Show Queen (ff)
4. Show Time (mm)
5. Show Dance (mm)

*Contemporary Series: Kapow!*

1. Out of Her League (fm with bisexual characters)
2. His Buxom Beauty (fm)
3. Craving His Spotlight (mm)
4. Her Pregnant Rival (ff)

*Contemporary Series: Farrellton Foster Family*

1. Betrayed (fm)
2. Forbidden (fm with bisexual characters)
3. Liability (ff)

*Contemporary Series: Margaret River TV: Boxed Set*

- Homage (fm with bisexual heroine)
- Uplift (ff with bisexual heroines)

*Contemporary Series: Merindah Park*

1. Merindah Park (fm)
2. Making Her Mark (fm with bisexual heroine)
3. Two Hearts Healing (fm)
4. Racetrack Royalty (fm)

*Contemporary Series: Rainbow Cove*

1. His Christmas Pearl (fm)
2. His Christmas Pride (mm)